Max and the Tom Cats

by Bobby Lynn Maslen
pictures by John R. Maslen

Scholastic Inc.
New York • Toronto • London • Auckland • Sydney • Mexico City • New Delhi • Hong Kong • Buenos Aires

Available Bob Books®:

Set 1: Beginning Readers — With consistent new sounds added gradually, your new reader is gently introduced to all the letters of the alphabet. They can soon say, "I read the whole book!®"

Set 2: Advancing Beginners — The use of three-letter words and consistent vowel sounds in slightly longer stories build skill and confidence.

Set 3: Word Families — Consonant blends, endings and a few sight words advance reading skills while the use of word families keep reading manageable.

Set 4: Complex Words — Longer books and complex words engage young readers as proficiency advances.

Set 5: Long Vowels — Silent e and other vowel blends build young readers' vocabulary and aptitude.

Bob Books® Collections:

Collection 1 — Includes Set 1: Beginning Readers and part of Set 2: Advancing Beginners

Collection 2 — Includes part of Set 2: Advancing Beginners and Set 3: Word Families

Collection 3 — Includes Set 4: Complex Words and Set 5: Long Vowels

Ask for Bob Books at your local bookstore, or visit www.bobbooks.com.

ISBN 0-545-02705-5

6 5 4 3 2   10 11/0

Printed in China   68
This edition first printing, September 2007

Six tom cats sit on the tiptop of a big wall.

The sun will set soon.

"E-ow, e-ow, e-ow,"
all of the cats call.
"Me-ow, me-ow, me-ow," they squall.

Max, who is six, sits up in a tree.

"Hey, cats," calls Max, "what do you see?"

But the cats' "Me-ow" is all they will tell.

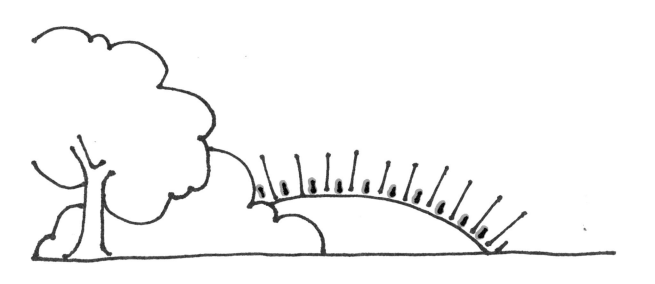

After a time
the sun did set.

As night fell, the cats called,
"Max, we see a big white ball."

Max looked up at the light as he sat in the tree. "What a wonderful sight," said he.

Then, as Max sat looking at the
big white moon, he suddenly saw
a man looking back at him.

The man in the moon saw six
cats and Max. "What a wonderful
sight tonight," said he.

Soon the bright light of the moon sat over them all.

Then the six tom cats did
begin to call and call and call.

"Me-ow, re-ow, bre-ow,"
they sang to Max
and to the man in the moon.

Max was glad
he was in the tree to see the
moonlight and to hear the song.

But at last the moon man
went out of sight. The song
was over until another night.

Go to bed, Max.

Go to bed, six tom cats.

Goodnight, Max.
Goodnight, Cats.

Goodnight, Moonlight.

The End

Book 8 adds:

x   –   six
sq –   squall

Silent e:
i - e   white